Colour Bears

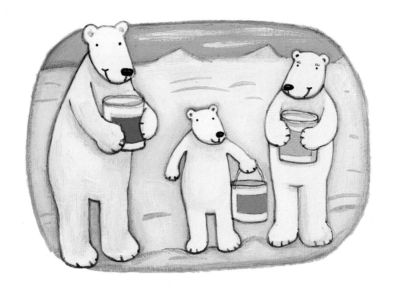

Written by Tasha Pym
Illustrated by Liz Pichon

Collins

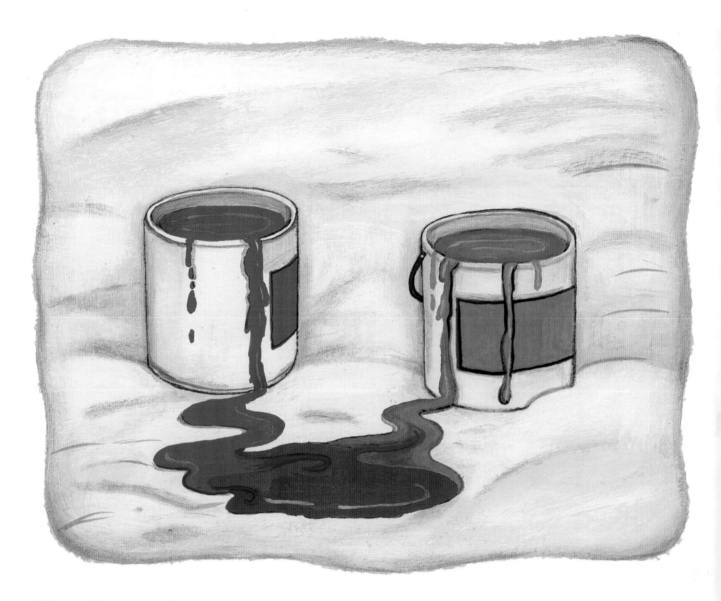

Red and blue make purple.

2

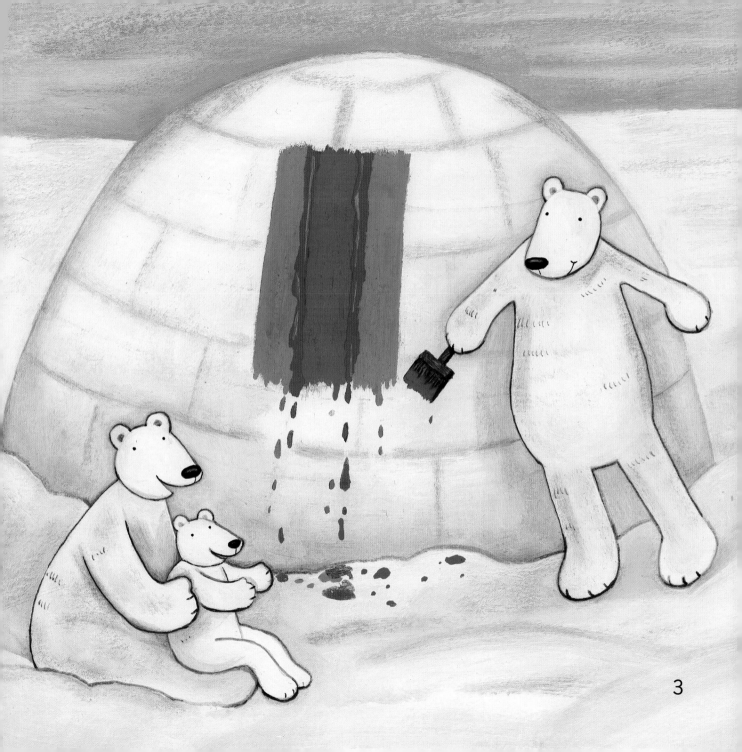

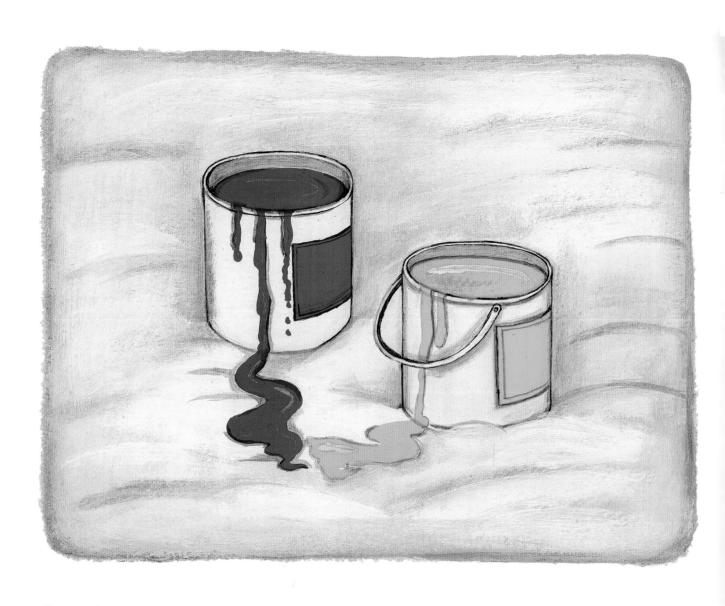

Red and yellow make ...

4

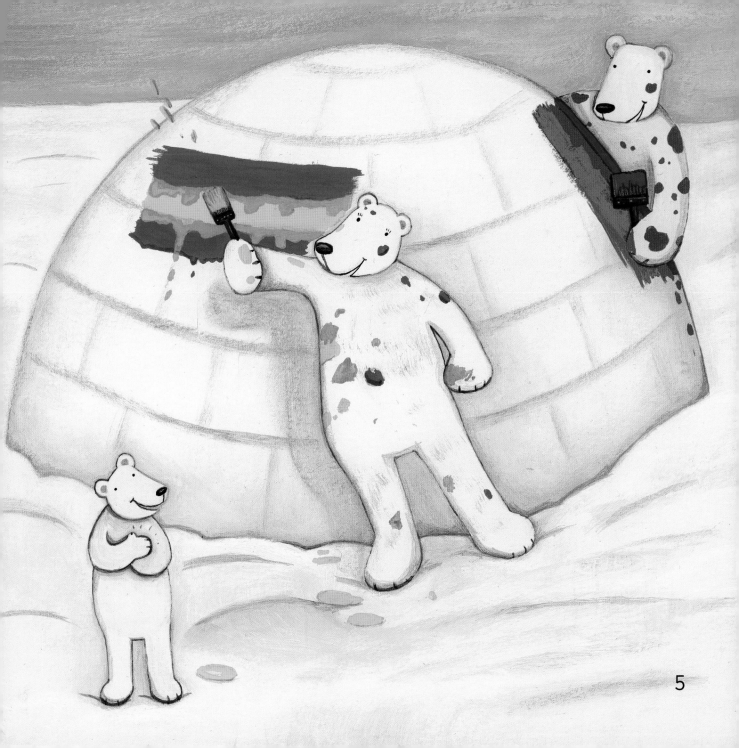

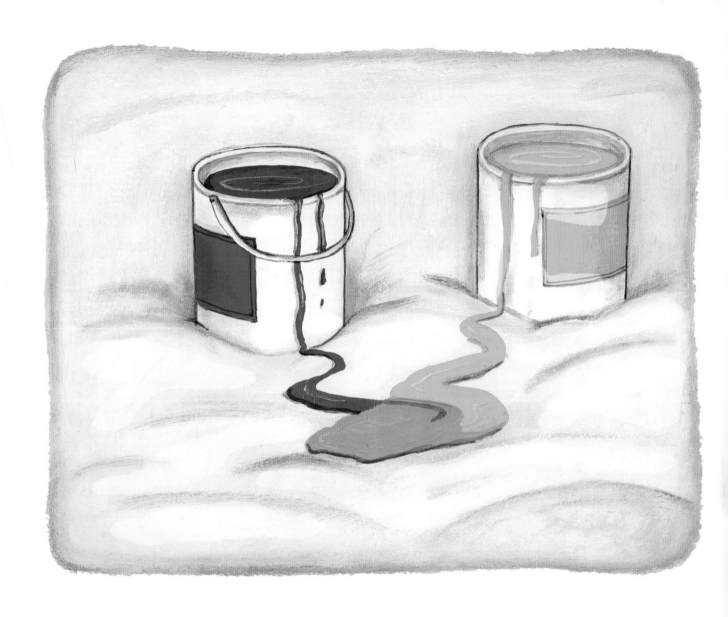

... orange.

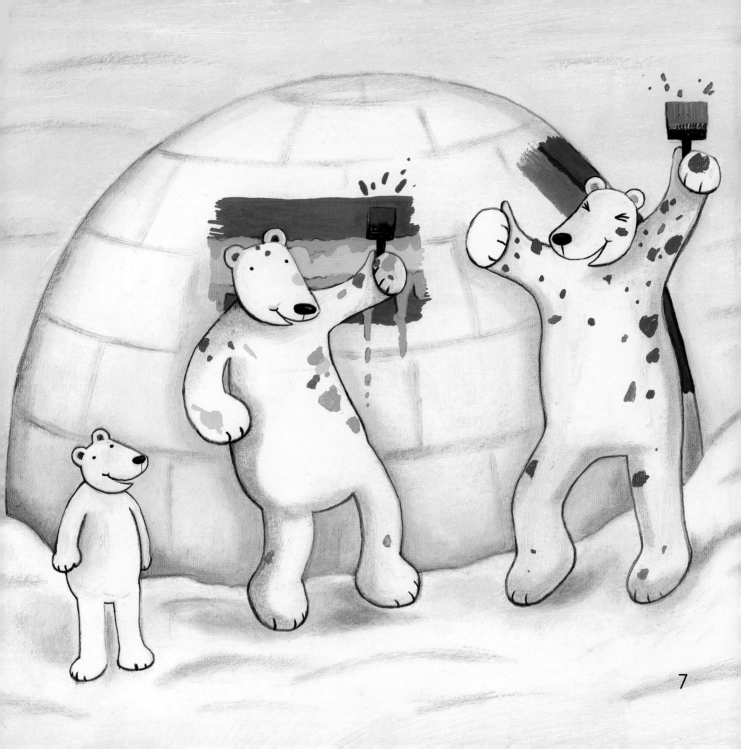

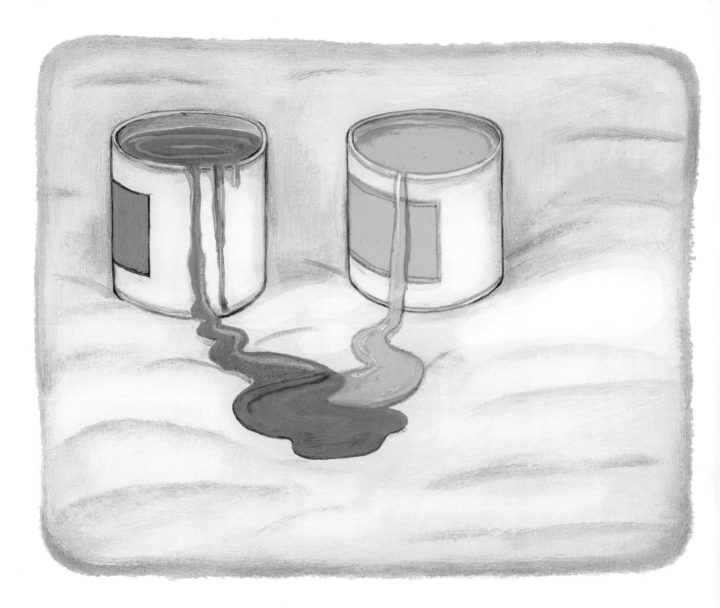

Blue and yellow make green.

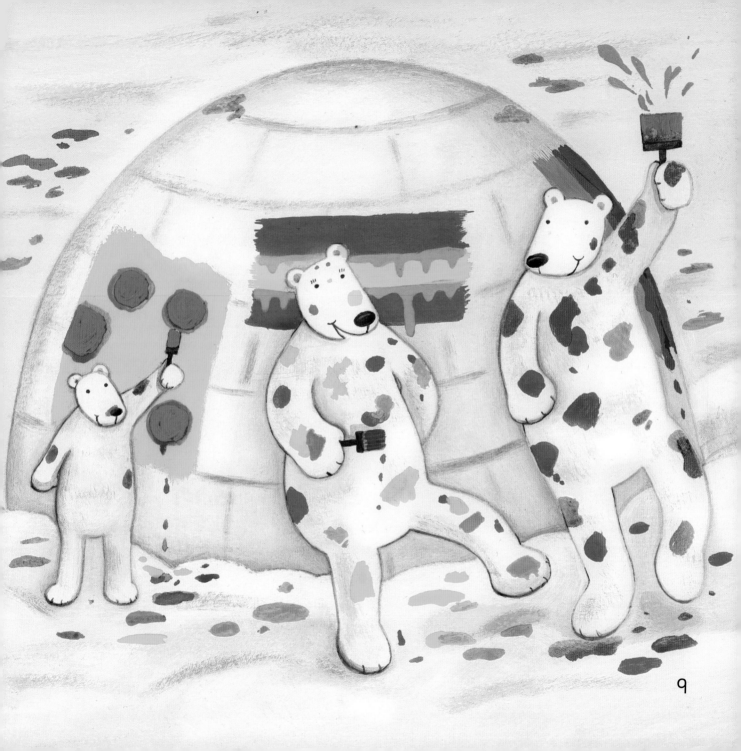

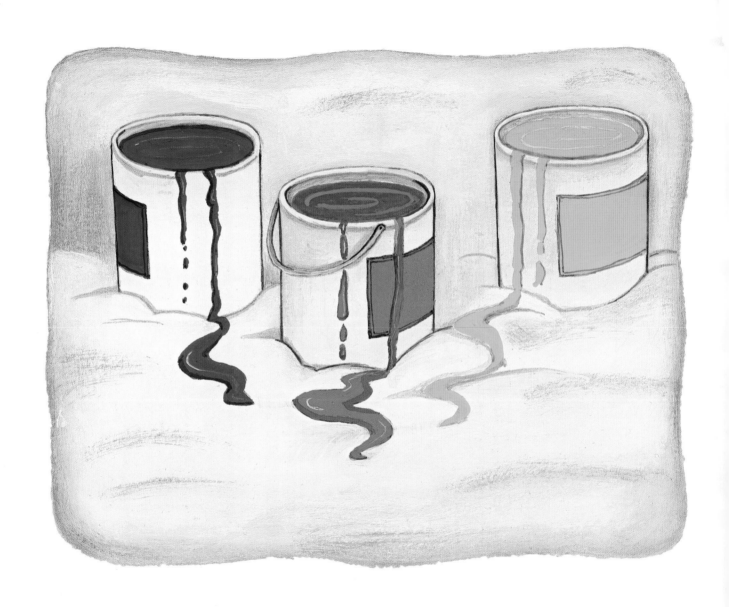

Red, blue and yellow make ...

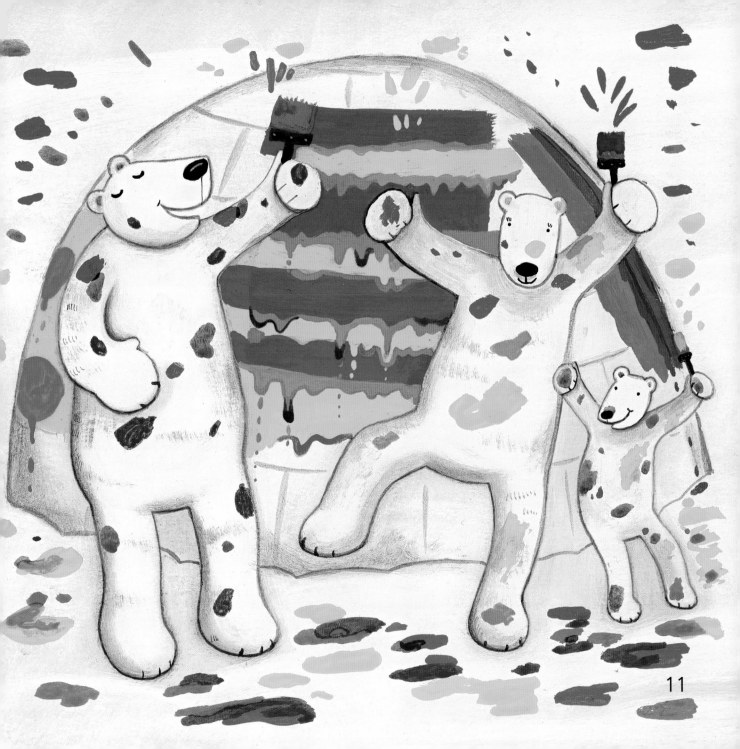

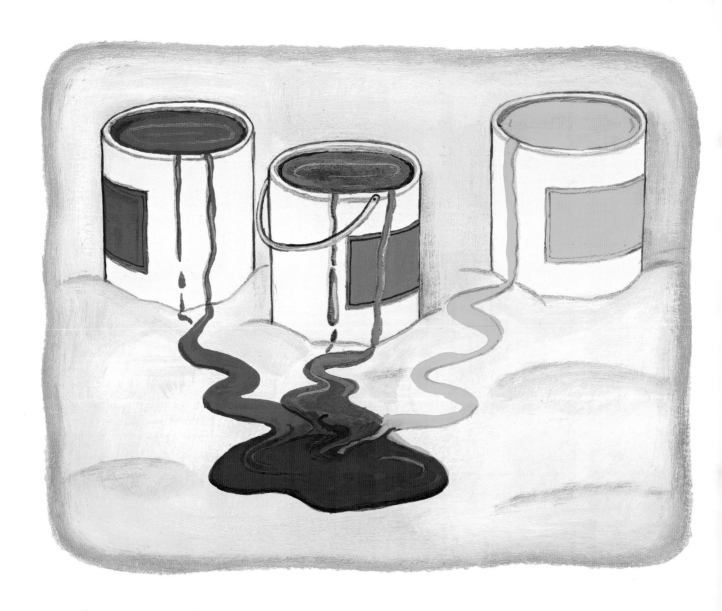

... brown!

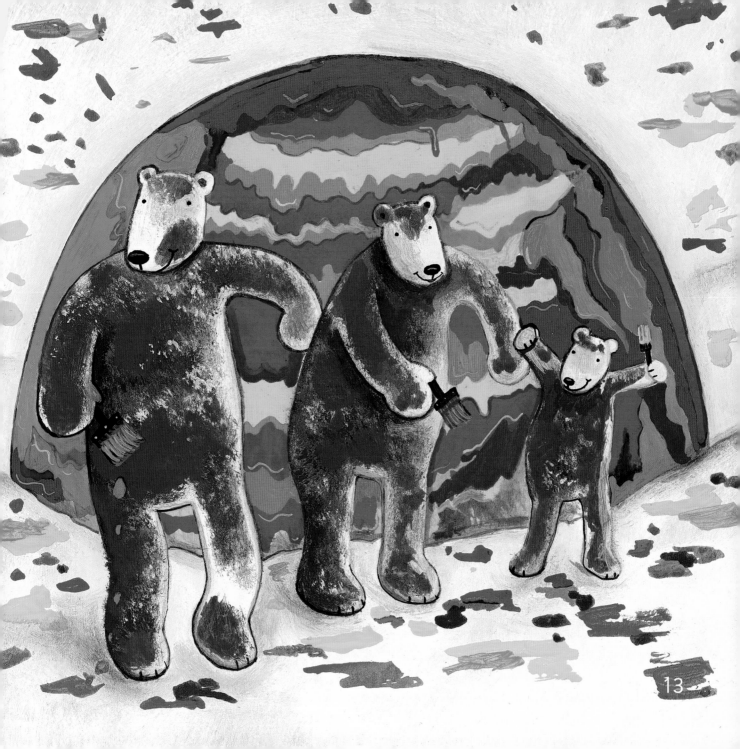

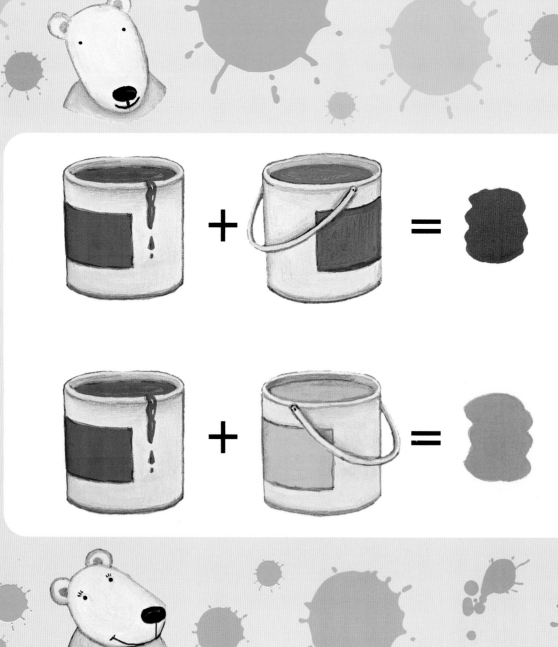